Q.S. ALERT

ISBN: 978-0-9556888-0-5

Copyright © R.W.Pearce 2008

Other books by the author:

Robert's Theories and Ideas
Published by Chipmunkapublishing

Bet for fun and win
Published by Best Global Publishing

INTRODUCTION

This is a true storey about a quantity surveyor, William Pitt, working in the construction industry in the 1990's. It starts with his employment working on the client's side, then moves on to him working for a contractor in London. He has health problems which makes life difficult and eventually leads to an early retirement.

This book mentions many contracts that William was involved with, without going into too much detail but highlighting points of interest. It is not too technical and is an easy read, consequently appealing to a wide range of readers.

We are all aware that the building industry is corrupt in many ways and there are a few underhand things going on in this book, which the reader should find of interest. To avoid any repercussions all names have been changed.

CHAPTER 1

Before we begin this book the author thought it was a good idea to describe the structure of the building industry which might be helpful to some people.

The Client
This is the most important person or body of people or organisation and therefore comes at the top of the structure. The client pays for the whole project and decides what he wants with the help of his team.

The Architect
In a traditional contract the client would appoint an architect who would be responsible for designing the building or proposed works and run the job on site issuing instructions to the contractor when necessary, certifying payments on account as work proceeds (these are called valuations and are usually monthly), issuing practical completion certificate when he is satisfied the works are substantially complete, issuing a defects list usually six months after practical completion, then a completion of making good defects certificate once he is satisfied the defects have been completed then a final certificate.

The Quantity Surveyor
The Q.S. is essentially the accountant to the works. He looks after the financial aspects. At pre contract stage he would give an estimate of the proposed works with the information supplied by the architect. If the client decides to go ahead with the works then traditionally the Q.S. would measure all the works from the drawings supplied by the architect, this is called 'taking off', then compile a Bill of Quantities which is essentially a pricing document for the

contractor to get the best price for the job which is usually the lowest.

About five or six main contractors are sent the Bill of Quantities for pricing and they are all returned to the Q.S. by a specified time and date. The Q.S. checks the Bill for any arithmetic errors and usually selects the lowest tender unless it is unreasonably low and in their opinion cannot carry out the works for that price, in which case he would encourage the contractor to withdraw his offer because nobody wants a contractor to go bankrupt especially the client as it would be costly engaging another contractor to complete the unfinished works.

When the works are in progress valuations are carried out usually on a monthly basis by the Q.S. who attends site and measures the work and issues a valuation certificate to the architect who authorises a payment on account. If the job was not financed periodically the contractor would have to borrow a lot of money, consequently the client makes a saving by this process.

At the same time as issuing a valuation the Q.S. does a cost report for the client indicating the expected final expenditure. This report is broken down into the various building elements and may contain contingency sums for works which cannot be reasonably evaluated at that stage.

The architect may well require an estimate or quotation from the Q.S. for proposed variations to the works not envisaged at tender stage. The Q.S. would require this information from the contractor. It is a generally accepted thing that the architect does not approach the contractor on financial aspects.

As the works precede sections of the valuations can be used by the Q.S. to compile the final account which is agreed with the contractor after practical completion. Sometimes the Q.S. and contractor do not agree with the cost of some elements of work and the final account is not actually agreed for a considerable length of time.

M&E Consultants
The mechanical and electrical works are specialist and the architect will call on these consultants for the original design and subsequent control of their area of work. They might be asked to advise the architect of suitable subcontractors who might be nominated to carry out the work.

The Main Contractor
This is the organisation that is responsible for carrying out the building work. Over twenty years ago they would directly employ a team of painters and decorators and have their own carpentry workshop, but more recently these works have been subcontracted out to **subcontractors.** At the very least they directly employ site agents responsible for the site, contracts managers, quantity surveyors and estimators who price the work.

Nominated Subcontractors
These subcontractors are nominated to carry out their specialist area of work. Nomination is not favoured these days because they know they've got the job and consequently there is no price control when tendering. They generally have a proven track record or might be

recommended to fix a certain product which the architect has put in his design.

Domestic Subcontractors
These days the main contractor will take on domestic subcontractors to carry out the bulk of the work like groundwork, brickwork, roofing, carpentry, labouring and painting and decorating. Very few are directly employed on the cards.

CHAPTER 11

William Pitt was attending an interview for a job as an assistant quantity surveyor with a small organisation in the private sector called Thomas Crapper and Partners in Colchester. It was his second interview that week, the first with a similar set up in the town, but they wanted him to be based at Chelmsford which is about twenty miles away and William wasn't keen on that offer.

He travelled in by bus and walked down the high street as far as the town hall then turned left into Blackberry Way and strolled down the hill for a few hundred yards until he arrived at St. John's House which was a quaint building about two hundred years old and held architectural interest. The private quantity surveyors rented part of this building from a solicitor who also occupied some floor space to carry out his work

He was led upstairs to the first floor and greeted by the partner Fred Smithers who didn't ask any technical questions, he just talked about what type of work the firm did and that there were three other offices in the practice, the main one at Beckenham where Mr.Thomas and Mr.Crapper the two head partners worked.

Apparently they all knew each other at the Home Office years ago and the partnership started when quantity surveying commissions were let out to tender in the private sector instead of being done in house. The two head partners saw the opportunity to make money having the advantage of inside contacts and branched out on their own.

Mr.Smithers liked the prospect of employing William because at thirty two he was mature and lacked experience so he wouldn't have to pay him much. Also he was keen to progress requesting day release to study for a degree which would be beneficial for both parties.

He had a specific role in mind for William and that was to manage all the measured term contracts in the office. They had a problem with these contracts in keeping up with the workload and were getting some nasty letters from the Property Services Agency.

William was not at all familiar with this type of work for he had just completed a H.N.D. in building which consisted of a limited amount of quantity surveying, mainly taking off quantities from drawings to compile bills of quantities.

William had decided to pursue a career in quantity surveying working for the clients interests because he had a mobility problem caused by arthritis and would find site management or even a contractor's quantity surveyor difficult due to the ground conditions.

Unfortunately he would find that as time progressed with his employment under Mr.Smithers he was prejudiced towards him because of his disability and stopped him from developing his skills and progressing in other areas of surveying which he would have preferred.

He had William earmarked for measured term work and very little else apart from a few boring final accounts which nobody else wanted to do. This was narrow minded, selfish and discriminative. Once his task had been completed and there was no more measured term work poor William was out the door.

Another major reason for Williams's employment came to light in due course which further emphasises the fact that he was used. Before he joined the firm they employed a freelance surveyor called Jimmy Sands who did a lot of work for the other offices as well. He was very good and quick at measured term work; he'd had years of experience.

But he was a naughty boy working on both sides of the fence. He would measure the work for Thomas Capper and get paid by the contractor as well for measuring for them. He also had an extension built on the side of his house by the contractor.

When the Property Services Agency (P.S.A.) got wind of this they gave Thomas Crapper an ultimatum, get rid of Jimmy Sands and clean up your act or loose all your contracts. So unbeknown to him William was pulled in as a front man to manage the mess that was left. He was a working manager measuring building and civil engineering and painting works.

Measured Term work was a way of measuring maintenance work of certain sites or group of buildings. The P.S.A. looked after R.A.F. and Army bases and employed a full time work force to manage all new build and maintenance works.

As time progressed it became a political issue that certain parts of these works should be let out to tender to the private sector. Quantity surveying duties followed this course, but the instruction of work to be carried out remained in house for many years until more recently when sites were let out as a complete package for all maintenance works for a period of time to prospective facilities management organisations.

The quantity surveying work was measured using a schedule of rates for various items of work. The work was measured on site by the quantity surveyor (Q.S.) when the P.S.A. officer had signed it off as being complete and the value of the work was built up using these rates and quantities. Then there was a percentage adjustment which varied monthly, this was termed the 'update'.

There was a schedule of rates for building and civil engineering works known as B&C.E., one for painting and decorating contracts, one for roads and paths and another for grounds maintenance.

The junior surveyors in the office were engaged in the grounds maintenance and painting and decorating because the scope of the work was far less complex than building and civil engineering which required a lot more building knowledge. Less experienced surveyors would progress later to these contracts if earmarked for this type of work.

During the early 1990's the system changed in that instead of employing an independent quantity surveyor to measure and agree the works with a contractors Q.S., self measure was introduced where the contractor measured his own work. A small percentage of these works orders were audited by the private Q.S. and if the accounts did not agree penalties were enforced on to the contractor.

Unfortunately this greatly reduced the workload of the private Q.S. and poor old William was now wishing he had not agreed to do get involved with this area of surveying.

This system only lasted two or three years before the schedule of rates was thrown out the window altogether. It was decided from senior management of the Home Office to appoint a reputable contractor to carry out the building maintenance works for a period of time which was usually three years.

The P.S.A. officer in charge of the site would issue a schedule of work known as a works order, as before, to the contractor who would give a quotation for carrying out the work. This system seemed crazy to William and many others because although the authorities were saving money by not employing surveyors to measure the work, there was no cost control which gave the contractor the scope to charge over the top for the works.

The schedule of rates was the best way of measuring building maintenance works and it's very unfortunate that it's no longer used. It costs the public sector more money because of the lack of cost control and many surveyors lost their jobs.

There were piles of work for William to sort out. They were at two R.A.F. bases, Wattisham and Bawdsey and an old contract which had finished two years previously at Colchester Garrison. The bulk of the work coming in was at R.A.F. Wattisham and there was already a surveyor working on this site for building maintenance, Ian White. He was a mature man in his early sixties and had worked with measured term contracts previously for the P.S.A. being directly employed and had a wealth of experience.

William didn't want to upset the apple cart and decided Ian was best suited here, although it was the best place to gain valuable experience he was not yet familiar with the schedule of rates and decided to work at Bawdsey with another old timer Fred Bates. Fred was about the same age as Ian and had had similar experience with the P.S.A. and Home Office, but he was a lot more laid back, which is realistically a polite term for lazy and enjoyed his drink, spending most of his time at a social club. They were both freelance surveyors and just booked the hours they worked to the partnership.

A perk to the job was being paid mileage, Bawdsey was about thirty miles away and William always drove while Fred had a snooze. Fred was not as knowledgeable as Ian but a lovely character that had an excellent sense of humour. He didn't produce much work but was good to have around. He measured with the contractor's senior surveyor and William partnered a new junior surveyor, Colin.

So it was a bit like the blind leading the blind because neither surveyor was had used the schedule of rates before which can be tricky until you become accustomed to it. Fred was a great help during the first few months, like Ian, who spent most of his time out the office, he knew the schedule inside out.

After a few months William and Colin became more proficient and needed less help, in fact they took over measuring all the maintenance works at Bawdsey and Fred was switched to measuring the old Garrison contract.

William found Colin to be pompous, he came from a wealthy background had a private education which didn't do him any favours because he had no natural ability. He mixed with those who had more money than sense and was a bit pig headed thinking he was a cut above the rest. William disliked him but was very careful to keep his views to himself, therefore maintaining a reasonable working relationship.

The work was quite low key and it took him to other sites like Old Felixstowe and Orfordness. The latter was a fascinating place, an island of off Orford which was only accessible by a P.S.A. ferry. It was very quiet having no residence and William thought it incredible when a rabbit came running up right beside him. It may well be that this rabbit hadn't seen a human before.

There was a very old listed timber lighthouse here and a job came through to refurbish it and replace rotten wood. It was quite a unique works order and every piece of timber replaced had to be measured. This structure is most likely to be the only one of its kind.

Bawdsey is a peninsular of the Suffolk coast and just across the water Old Felixstowe is clearly visible. Bawdsey manor is the main feature on the site which is a beautiful building built in the 1800's. It was owned by a wealthy business man who dealt in stocks and shares and when he made a good deal he would invest the money in the building by adding extensions to it.

Up to the late 1990's this lovely building was used as accommodation for R.A.F. personnel and it backs onto the sea. At the front is a small drive and beyond that is a large grassed area.

The works orders on this site were generally of small value. A lot of them were for timber repairs where a section of window for example had gone rotten and a piece had to be spliced in and decorated. The repair of concrete paving was another common item and the shower rooms were frequently having repairs to them, for some reason the shower units quite often had to be replaced.

There was a much larger order which came in to refurbish a pair of cottages on the site. This seemed a bit pointless because although they were run down and in desperate need of work being carried out on them, nobody actually lived there and they weren't used for any other purpose.

But it was the P.S.A.'s responsibility to keep the site to a reasonable standard and if they had money left over at the end of the financial year they would look around for ways of spending it because if they didn't their allocation the following year would be reduced.

At the rear of the manor was a lovely sunken garden and to one side a dilapidated lemony stood. An associate in the office had carried out an estimate to restore it but it was decided that the job was too expensive so it was shelved.

There were a few outbuildings; there was a store for R.A.F. basic materials and a small shop. The contractor had a small hut and yard for materials. The majority of the buildings appeared not to be used. So the work here was low key and although it was a lovely place William found it a bit boring.

CHAPTER 111

William Pitt acquired a job in Kings Lynn; it was a refurbishment job for the Halifax Building Society. The term job is used in construction terms to mean a contract whether it is new build, refurbishment or alterations to an existing building. A Q.S. would have several jobs running at the same time, the amount depending on the size and complexity of the contracts and the ability and experience of the individual.

William was overseen by an associate of Thomas Crapper who had very little input which suited him because it gave him the opportunity to gain experience and the freedom to measure the works without somebody looking over his shoulder all the time, which can be very frustrating.

The contract value was £850,000, but this was going to be exceeded because of ground problems not envisaged at tender stage. The contract had been negotiated with the contactor using the rates from another Bill of Quantities on a similar job with a small percentage addition.

The ground problem was discovered when the floor slab was broken out. Because the building was on the coast the water table level was high and ground beams had to be constructed for a stable base before the proposed works could be carried out.

The building was listed and certain features had to be maintained. One of these was a beautiful timber staircase which was expertly refurbished by craftsman. Also a few sash windows had to be carefully rebuilt and some of the existing still had the original Victorian glass panes.

Kings Lynn was a two hour drive in the company pool car and William found it very tiring with his arthritis complaint. He measured the provisional works with a contractor's junior surveyor who was not honest and had an annoying habit of trying to add on extra lengths of superlux and vermiculux boarding when he thought he could get away with it. This made Williams job more difficult and he had to be on his guard all the time. Occasionally there was the odd heated exchange of words when the contractor's surveyor wasn't playing ball.

By 2.00pm both surveyors were hungry and had lunch at a pub which was walking distance. It was generally accepted that the contractor's surveyor pays for the lunch which he did and claimed back from his employer with a receipt. Private surveyors have to be careful not to accept gifts from contactors in case they form a bribe. But William was happy to accept lunch, he found this acceptable but would never accept a bribe or what is more commonly known as a brown envelope.

William was assigned this job about a third into the works which suited him because he found groundwork physically difficult to cope with and on his first visit they had the rear steel staircase in position so there were no ladders to encounter. Parking was not a problem as the building faced Tuesday market where there was ample room providing his weekly visit was not on market day.

After three months the contract was completed and handed over. An extension of time had been granted and the works had been accelerated at an agreed percentage addition which meant that the contractor was reimbursed for working some trades out of sequence which has a cost implication. The enhanced cost was agreed by the client so he could get his building earlier, a situation which sometimes occurs in building works. Obviously the client has to weigh up this additional cost with the income he would get having his building at an earlier date.

Then the final account had to be prepared and agreed with the contractor. William was familiar with preparing final accounts because in his measured term work each works order had to be agreed individually and was in itself a final account although Kings Lynn was substantially larger.

William met a senior surveyor to agree the final account who was much more experienced and his associate offered very little help, in effect this job had been dumped on him. But William was intelligent and knew the job well although he had not been involved at pre contract stage the final account was prepared by him with all the provisional sums and quantities omitted and the Architects instructions measured.

A particular Building Society was one of Thomas Crapper's major clients and only had a few carefully selected employees working on their contracts because they formed a large chunk of their income. Another client in the private sector was a Bank, but William had not been engaged on any of these contracts. A large proportion of their work came from the public sector like the P.S.A. for defence, education for schools and councils for public buildings and housing.

One of the defence jobs was at R.A.F. Fylingdales in Yorkshire which is our early warning system. Because of the Official Secrets Act the writer cannot give any details of this job. William was involved with this job and travelled up there to meet the contractor's surveyor once a month for valuations.

Valuations are a payment on account as work proceeds, nothing is really finalised until the final account is signed. He stayed overnight at Pickering and Whitby and claimed back expenses from the firm. Once again, he was overseen by the same associate who was ultimately responsible. After the contract was completed the final account was prepared and agreed. The contractor's surveyor was very reasonable and didn't pull any fast ones.

Another contract William got involved with was the refurbishment and alterations of Army accommodation in Colchester. He was not involved until the works had been completed and assisted in the measurement of architect's instructions to form the final account.

The contract value was about £2 million, and there were a lot of variations to measure as a large proportion of the bill of quantities were provisional. This is quite often the case with this type of work because it's not until you enter the properties and start work that the full scope can be envisaged. Also it's very costly and time consuming to do a full pre contract survey.

* * * * * * * * *

When the measured term work for the P.S.A. had almost dried up, the partner told William to go to their London office to meet the partner there, he was not told why.

He had a meeting with the partner who had a measured term contract using the national schedule of rates, which is mainly for the alteration and refurbishment of houses, for a London Borough. He was to be overseen by an associate in London. There were two contracts lasting about two years, one was for external works and the other internal and external refurbishment and alterations to the council's houses.

It soon became apparent that William had been called in to sort out a bit of a mess. The Borough's architect had kicked up a bit of a fuss that the previous surveyor was too young and inexperienced, which was probably true.

The main contractor was paid with monthly valuations which were difficult for William because it meant physically measuring the work to date, unlike working with a bill of quantities where everything is measured beforehand and a percentage agreed. This meant at least two trips to London a week which was tiring. The remainder of the week was spent writing up the work carried out to date which would be carried forward to the final account.

Also the schedule of rates was entirely different to the P.S.A. schedule and took a while to get used to, but after a while William found the schedule easier because it consisted of various block items which included several items of work.

The contract for internal and external alterations and refurbishment took up most of William's time. The contract with the Local Authority stated that all the quantity surveying duties should be carried out by Thomas Crapper, unlike the P.S.A. contracts which were jointly measured with the contractor. In this situation a contractor would usually employ a Q.S. to keep an eye on things. Plus the fact it would be financially beneficial to do so because he could pick up on extras which might have been overlooked. But the contactor was only a small concern and didn't employ any Q.S.'s; in fact they let all the works to a subcontractor and took 5% of the value of the work.

This meant William had his work cut out. The main contractor employed a contracts manager who liaised with the architect and the subcontractor and also met William to agree the valuations. He didn't do any measuring; he had no quantity surveying experience anyway, but compared the valuations with his costs. It was not an ideal partnership but it served its purpose and gave William a lot of freedom to measure the works as he saw fit.

The houses they were working on were very run down and quite often before they could survey them a team of people were called in to dispose of needles and such like that drug takers had used. They worked on about five properties at the same time and the value of the work in each was £40-£90 thousand. The scope of the work varied but more often than not the internals were completely gutted and refitted to the architects design. There were no extensions or such like added, just a major refurbishment of the existing building.

The other contract was entirely different. Although Thomas Crapper's contractual obligations were the same, the contractor on this contract had a Q.S. who generally had the external works measured before meeting William so all he had to do was check the measurements, a piece of cake really. This was also measured on the national schedule of rates and the value of the works was a lot less. These works consisted of roofing, concrete and stonework repairs, pointing of brickwork, timber repairs and external decorations.

William quite often met the architect on site and got on reasonably well with him. Because he had complained about the previous surveyor it was the associate's opinion that he would be keen to get on with him as he wouldn't want to get a reputation for being over fussy about who he had working on his contracts.

There was not the time to do a full initial survey on the properties because the contractor was in place and needed to start work straight away. So it was all a bit piece meal, the architect got the keys to the dwelling and wrote out longhand a brief schedule to get the works underway. Then as work proceeded he would give further written instructions.

Occasionally the contactor would come across items of work that needed to be carried out and they had no written instruction and the architect was not available to attend site. So they would contact him and he would give a verbal instruction so as not to hold up the works which he would later confirm in writing himself or sign the contractors written statement of what he had done.

This works reasonably well providing it's kept up to date and the verbal instructions are signed of and included in an architect's instruction at regular intervals because it's the surveyors brief not to pay for any work that hasn't been instructed. The problem is when work gets covered up before the architect gets a chance to see it, or items get forgotten until a later date when it's difficult to establish what has been done.

The contracts manager kept on telling William that the architect was bent, but William held an open mind. Providing he did his job properly he had nothing to worry about. But there were one or two instances that concerned him.

For example a whole flank side if a house had recently been pointed and the contracts manager claimed they had done it and were waiting for an instruction. Now this could have been done before they attended site, William didn't know, but sure enough an instruction for the work soon followed. So the contractor may not have been entirely honest either, but they are always on the lookout for extras and love it when they get paid for something they haven't done.

William was sure there was something dodgy going on when the contracts manager told him that there were two immigrants who couldn't speak English working on one of their jobs. Apparently the architect had told them to employ them and even had the cheek to tell them how much they should be paid.

So there was something not quite right all round otherwise the contractor wouldn't have entertained such an arrangement. William told the partner in the office and even Mr.Thomas when he came to the office who said if there was anything going on he would write to the director of the building company, but he didn't. The partner merely said it's difficult to grass up your client. But the architect met his day and his services were disposed with although William didn't hear of the details somebody must of got wind of something because he went very quickly and it wasn't due to lack of work.

CHAPTER 1V

The 1980's saw a boom in the construction industry under Margaret Thatcher's government and nobody could see an end to it. Builders of all trades had plenty of work and were well paid, in fact such was the demand for labour there was a shortage and certain trades, notably plastering, charged very high rates.

Inevitably this came to an abrupt end and many contractors and subcontractors were owed money but didn't get paid. Many went bankrupt and lost everything including their houses. Recession had hit the industry and being the major employer of people in the U.K. it affected the whole country.

In fact globally economic growth was hardly existent if at all, in fact we had not seen such a downturn since the 1930's. It lasted about ten years but seemed to go on for ever and many doubted it would ever recover. It was extremely difficult to find work and if you were lucky enough to find it the pay was low with usually a short term contract with no prospects.

Very few organisations were prepared to take on employees full time with a reasonable contract of employment; in fact many took on employment agency staff who only offered works one week at a time with no holiday or sick pay.

Thomas Crapper had made two or three redundancies and in 1994 it was Williams turn to go due to lack of work. It was very disappointing for him, he had put a lot of effort into measured term work which had fallen by the way and always worked hard to produce his best. He received a small redundancy package for five and a half years service and spent his last month desperately trying to find a new job, which wasn't easy.

At a later date William found out that his redundancy was not above board. To make somebody redundant there must be no work, or similar work, that the person can do. But Thomas Crapper employed an architect's son who had limited experience soon after the event.

William rather expected that there was a motive; the prospect of getting work through his father for doing the 'good' deed, although there was nothing good about it at all, in fact it was very underhand. They also took on another Q.S. who had been studying for his degree in the same class as William, so he was of similar experience.

Furthermore, a building surveyor based at their head office was sent down to work at the Colchester office and did so for several years. William was quite disgusted by this and did consider taking legal advice, but one thing led to another and he didn't get round to it.

William was very fortunate to find other work within a week at Rutland Council through an employment agency. The hours were nine till five but it meant a long commute from Colchester every day because the Borough of Rutland was so far away. He found it very tiring getting up at 5.30am to leave at 6.30am and arriving at home 7.30 to 8.00pm. He had a ten minute walk to catch the bus to North Station, and then caught the 7.05am to Liverpool Street. He slept most of the way then went on the underground and finally had a twenty minute walk to the office. .

William was now working on the contractor's side which he found very interesting and rewarding. The money was better because he had not previously received a pay rise for two and a half years, so things were not too bad for him apart from the travelling. Rutland Construction was a council company which had to show a profit in order to exist.

They did this with reasonable ease for the first three or four years William was there. They tendered for work from Rutland Building and Design in competition with the private sector and won enough work to keep a small office running. The work was either for one of the nineteen neighbourhoods that Rutland was divided into or for education with schools.

There were five quantity surveyors, eight site agents and a contracts manager working in a small prefabricated hut. Fortunately the site agents spent very little time in the hut, they were out on site running their jobs, because conditions were very cramped.

Three estimators worked in another council building a few hundred yards away. The contracts manager had only been engaged a few weeks before William arrived, he was a very pleasant genuine man in his early fifties. Only two of the surveyors enjoyed the benefit of full time employment with a permanent contract with the holiday and sick pay. One of them had been with Rutland for nearly forty years, the other just seven years.

William and the other two surveyors were employed through an agency on an hourly rate with only one weeks notice, no holiday or sick pay. It was a sign of the difficult times the construction industry was going through, it was an employers market.

In fact it worked out cheaper if Rutland employed them directly, but they didn't want the long term commitment. Furthermore, there was a dodgy deal going on between senior management and the agencies where they got a cut of the difference of what they charged Rutland and paid their employees.

All subcontractors carrying out work for the council had to be approved and put on a list unless it was specialist work. They had to have a good proven track record and their previous five years accounts had to be approved. They also had to hold £5 million public liability insurance.

William was told he only had six months work, once the job he was working on had finished then he was down the road. But at least he was working, unlike thousands of others. The job he was given was called Dedham House, which was one of the neighbourhoods. It was a painting and decorating contract with associated repairs and had a contract sum of £850,000.

It was considered to be more difficult to run than the usual contracts in the office because it was not back to back, that is it wasn't priced the same as the subcontractors with a percentage addition for profit. But William soon found this was to their advantage because the sums of money for painting the blocks of flats were larger than they were paying out.

The only downfall was that the rates for repairs were considerably lower. But fortunately the provisional sums they had for repairs were much higher than that expended, which increased their profit margins.

There were several blocks of flats to redecorate externally and internally in the stairwell areas only. On this type of contract it was better to let the decorating and scaffolding to the same subcontractor so they took responsibility for any extra hire charges if there were any unnecessary time delays which did not warrant an extension of time.

Also, from experience it was learnt not to separate the repairs and decorating between two subcontractors because this can create problems if the repairs are not carried out to fall in line with the decorating schedule, which would probably result in the decorators putting in a loss and expense claim for working out of sequence, or working non-productively.

One of the items in the bill of quantities was to chemically strip the internal paintwork on the walls in the stairwell area. This is because a year or two earlier Rutland had a terrible incidence on a block of flats where the internal walls caught fire and it spread very quickly at about a metre per second chasing a poor man who eventually died. This is known as a flash fire caused by too many layers of paint on the walls.

A chemical called paramose was recommended for stripping the paint which is highly toxic and burns the skin. So the areas had to be tented out to protect the residents and visitors to the blocks. Because of the dangerous nature of the work a risk assessment had to be drawn up by the subcontractor for approval before the works could proceed.

This item of work went according to plan but unfortunately on another contract which had been let to the private sector things did not go so well and they had not adequately allowed for all the extra work in tenting out and unfortunately went bankrupt.

William had a site agent on the job called Tim who was very experienced having worked for the Council for over thirty years as a painter. They also employed another freelance agent because the job was so large and spread over a big area.

The team worked well together and every month they had to attend a progress meeting with the client, architect and quantity surveyor. The contracts manager did not attend these meetings and it was left very much up to William to be answerable for any queries. This was very good experience for him but quite stressful.

After a few weeks the freelance agent was moved onto another contract in the office and a new assistant agent was appointed. When this agent moved on Tim said to William that he thought the contracts manager was using Dedham House as a training ground for agents. William agreed, but it made things more difficult for the job keep on changing the agent, as soon as they got settled in and used to the contract they were shifted off, which was frustrating, particularly for Tim.

William's counterpart, the client's quantity surveyor, was a horrible mean man who kept on cutting down the value of the valuations. His name was Peter Harvey and he gained the nickname 'halve it Harvey'. He had previously worked as a subcontractor's surveyor for the architect Jimmy Walsh who was a plasterer by trade.

They were good mates, but Jimmy was a much more pleasant person. How on earth he got the job as an architect with his background God only knows, but he got on well with Tim and had an annoying habit of trying to put William down saying things like it was amazing he managed to get the job he had, when in actual fact it was even more amazing he held down his job which was full time with all the benefits of holidays, sickness and a pension. So he was a bit full of himself really and rumour had it he was once a millionaire having made his money as a plastering subcontractor for another Council.

Dedham House was the largest neighbourhood and the contract covered a big area. William had no transport and although there were a lot of busses they rarely went in the right direction and they were time consuming.

Tim was very helpful offering to take William out at regular intervals around the site to view the works progress and discuss any problems that had occurred. There were several blocks of flats and many individual houses scattered over a wide area on this contract. It was probably due to the geographic nature of the work that the subcontractor fell behind time on progress.

At the beginning of a contract a plan of work is drawn up with time scales. This is done by the subcontractor and submitted to the main contractor for approval then to the client.

Every month when the valuations are carried out a progress report is drawn up compared to the original plan of work. This is to monitor the progress of the works and highlight where the work is not being completed in a reasonable time. When this occurs it can be addressed at an early stage and discussed with the subcontractor so they can adjust their labour strength accordingly.

Alternatively, if unforeseen problems have been encountered not envisaged at tender stage an extension of time to the contract period might be applied for and warranted.

Despite falling behind time for no good reason other than lack of labour, the neighbourhood asked if Rutland Construction would like three more blocks of flats to be added onto the contract. They were prepared to take these three blocks out of a future proposed contract.

This would be subject to the price being agreed. Both William and Tim were keen on this additional work because it would mean an extension of time of a month or two which would give William more work. Tim was also looking for more work to increase his pension rights.

William drew up the documents based on those submitted to him by the client and gave them to the subcontractor for pricing. It would generally be the accepted thing that the additional work would be priced at pro-rata to the original works and the surveyors would be looking at it on this basis.

This means that the number of units in the additional blocks would be compared to those in the original works and a price calculated on a proportionate basis with an addition for some preliminary items like supervision, water for the works and the disposal of waste materials. Scaffolding was measured as a block item in with the painting and decorating.

The subcontractor came back with a much bigger price than expected, which is not surprising really because they were not in competition with any other contractors.

William tried to negotiate them down pointing out their prices in the original tender. This made a little difference, but not much. So William added on his percentage and submitted the document to the client.

Tim and William went along to a meeting with Brian Harvey to discuss the price and as expected his reaction was it wasn't a reflection of the original tender. William explained that the subcontractor's price was higher than expected and he was unable to negotiate it down to a reasonable level.

So as expected Harvey recommended that the neighbourhood should not accept the price and the works didn't go ahead. It was also apparent that the subcontractor's original tender was too low and they saw the extra work as an opportunity to pull some money back, but they got a bit too greedy and lost out altogether in the end.

Once the scaffolding was up on a block or the dwellings were otherwise accessible, the architect carries out his survey writing out all necessary instructions for repairs. This is the usual procedure on all contracts. The subcontractor then carries out his painting works when the repairs have been completed.

Quite often some repair work is missed and it is a contractual requirement that no extra works should be done unless authorised with an architect's instruction. If there is a good working relationship between the architect and the contractor, which in this case there was, the architect would agree verbally to extra work so as not to disrupt the progress of the works if he is unable to attend site at that particular time.

These verbal instructions are later confirmed in writing on an instruction.

On this type of work at the end of a job there is usually a list of works the subcontractor has claimed to have carried out without an instruction.

Really contractually he shouldn't carry out any work unless instructed, but sometimes it's necessary. This becomes a particular problem when the works are covered up. William had difficulty in agreeing with the subcontractor exactly what extra work they had done.

For example when a concrete sill needed repairing it was almost impossible to determine the extent of the repair, if any, after the sill had been painted with masonry paint. William was keen to be fair but at the end of the day the subcontractor had ample time to inform the site agent of the necessary work so he could authorise it acting on the architect's behalf.

At a later date William was introduced to the subcontractor who claimed to have carried out a lot of concrete repairs on this job for which he hadn't been paid. He was hoping William might put some pressure on the subcontractor to pay him, but it was very much his word against theirs and also there had not been a lot of concrete repairs instructed.

Furthermore, this was the first time William had met this man and he was directly responsible to the subcontractor, not to Rutland, so he was very reluctant to get involved in his dispute because there was no contractual link.

After three or four months the work was completed and a practical completion certificate was issued. The works ran over the original contractual contract period, but an extension of time was granted for this on the grounds of adverse weather conditions. A record of the days lost due to weather had been carefully kept to substantiate this. The next and final stage as far as William was concerned with his employment was the preparation and agreement of the final account.

Soon after Dedham House started on site William was given another job to run. This was a totally different contract and one which was new to the office. It was for the refurbishment and renewal of water tanks in high rise blocks. This was completely new to William but it turned out to be a piece of cake.

William selected the subcontractor who had the lowest tender and had a meeting with the contract administrator on site. This subcontractor withdrew stating that an inexperienced estimator had priced the job and there was no way he could make it pay. So the next lowest was taken on which created a bit of a problem because Rutland's tender was based on the previous lower tender.

Fortunately there was not a great deal of difference in the cost of the tanks, which was the bulk of the work. Obviously the two subcontractors had based their prices on the same supplier. The main difference was in the plumbing costs which were provisional and had been over measured. So things worked out quite well in the end and Rutland made a reasonable profit.

There was something a bit fishy going on with this contract and other similar contracts. It is generally not acceptable for the architect or contract administrator to specify a particular product or manufacturer because it's not in the interest of competition. If they knew their product was stated in the documents then naturally they would inflate its price because there would be no worries of losing the job to another firm.

If the architect particularly wants something on his job then they state it in the documents and say 'or similar approved', which is generally the accepted way of getting around the problem. Then the contractor is free to obtain alternative prices to submit in his tender providing it meets the architect's approval.

The documents specified a type of tank lining which had only one manufacturer and a very limited number of suppliers who obviously had similar prices for this particular product. This type of lining was a relatively new system which had strict installation guidelines and it could be seen that the contract administrator might have been persuaded to use this product by a backhander.

The auditors were called in and had a meeting with William who had nothing to do with preparing the documents. They had initially got the wind up because the lowest contractor had withdrawn before starting. Once they established it was the estimators who put the tender together based on the contractor's submission, they apologised to William for taking up his time. They may well have taken the matter further because the estimating department had a visit from them and at a later date the contract administrator resigned.

CHAPTER V

After William had been working for Rutland for four or five months he had cracked the nut and proved himself to be a good at his job. It was at this time that British Rail was offering a cut price three months rail ticket, which would make a considerable saving. But to warrant it worthwhile William needed to ensure he would have employment for this period.

He approached a senior manager who was based nearby and explained the situation. A couple of weeks later the contracts manager called him into his office and offered him the choice of one of two new jobs expressing that he was disappointed that William had gone above his head to obtain this extra work. It would have been courteous to approach him first but he didn't have much clout and William desperately wanted a quick result, which he got.

The new job was the external painting and decorating of a school called Wilson Marriage. William was delighted, for he had paved the way for future work. He purchased the cut price rail ticket knowing his employment for this period had been secured. There was also a little bit of lead roofing to be done and William got three quotes and gave it to the cheapest who was much lower than the others, but it was the roofers first job for Rutland and all they wanted to do was get their foot in the door. They did a good job and were easy to get on with and went on to do several other sizable jobs for Rutland.

The painting work was carried out by a well known subcontractor who had completed many similar jobs before. Their Q.S., Ginger, had previously worked for

Rutland on a freelance basis but left under a cloud when the recession hit hard and they reduced his hourly rate.

He had a bit of a chip on his shoulder and although he was good at his job he was very persistent on certain issues and could be a nuisance. He would try and find a loophole in the documents and use it to make money. One can't blame him for doing this; it's his job to make money for his organisation.

But it was his manner which was unfavourable; he used to get fired up and angry if he didn't get his way. His temperament had been an issue before with Rutland, he got annoyed with the full timers who were now enjoying better benefits whereas a year or two previously it had been the other way round, but that's the way the cookie crumbles.

Sure enough there was an issue on this job where William and Ginger came to blows. It was stated in the preambles of the documents that for health and safety purposes no children should be present in a classroom when burning off of paintwork is taking place. This was disruptive to the men's work pattern because they couldn't do this item of work when the classroom was occupied, so it took a lot of organising with the site agent and headmistress to make certain rooms available at the right time.

Inevitably this caused a delay in the progress of their work and sometimes men were standing idle unable to work because the classrooms were occupied. So Ginger wanted to submit day work sheets to claim back these lost hours. They even had a meeting with Rutland's contracts manager to discuss the issue.

But William stood firm on his argument that everything had been clearly stated in the contract documents and consequently the subcontractor was fully aware of his obligations and should have adequately allowed for it in his tender. So William didn't pay for the hours they claimed to have wasted, but it was all a headache because Ginger kept on and on about it.

The overall building manager was based a couple of miles away at the councils main depot. He was in charge of all the building works including the maintenance contracts the direct labour had.

His secretary was a blond in her late twenties and it was well known he was having a fling with her. She took advantage of this and arranged for a couple of electricians to rewire her house. This was booked down to a job which was quite easy to do providing everybody keeps quiet. But somebody grassed her up and she was given the push. A couple of months later she was seen pulling pints in a run down pub, so her relationship didn't do her any favours in the long term.

Some time later this manager was invited out for an evening's entertainment by a builder. They finished up at a hotel where everything was laid on including an overnight stay. Whether it was all a set up or things didn't work out as planned is not known, but the next day the contractor grassed him up to the director and he was fired.

About the same time the under manager that William had approached for more work was under scrutiny. A previously employed site agent who had taken early retirement had submitted a full report implicating him on several fiddles.

The agent was an outspoken pig if a man which was probably why the council were making life difficult for him forcing him to make an exit. It took a few months then eventually the manager was pushed out, but not before he had bought himself an expensive four by four jeep claiming it was paid for by a win on the lottery.

The introduction of computers has made fiddling more difficult, or at least greatly reduced it in the opinion of many. But it still goes on and brown envelopes are quite a common occurrence in the building game. One particular Council is reputed to have had a dreadful problem in this area.

There was a court case which was well advertised in the Building Magazine involving a surveyor and contractor. William couldn't believe what he was reading, the judge was so naïve. It was held that it was pure coincidence that the surveyor and contractor were on the same flights and stayed at the same five star hotel at an exotic expensive destination.

The probability of this occurring without being pre planned is extremely high, far too high to be a coincidence. If you can get away with that then you can get away with almost anything. It was not in William's nature to accept bribes and nobody had approached him any way, he preferred to sleep at night.

The estimating department were busy preparing their largest tender and the managers were keen to win it for political reasons. It was called 'Craig Estate' and involved a major refurbishment of several blocks of flats including the installation of lifts, which is very expensive and unfortunately leaseholders had to pay a portion of the cost.

Some had a problem in paying and a few took desperate steps and left their property with no forwarding address, which is a shame and in Williams opinion the system was unfair because even if the leaseholders did not want the lifts installed the council still went ahead regardless.

At the adjudication stage which is when senior management meet to discuss the tender they decided to not add anything on for head office costs because they had no rent to pay on the councils property which would be an advantage over the private sector and make their tender more competitive.

So they submitted a tender of £12 million and won the job by £2 million, which is a very uncomfortable margin and a serious question had to be answered, could they afford to do the job at this price? The market is the best indicator which suggested the council would make a loss, which is what eventually happened. But the neighbourhood were keen for Rutland to do the work because they were considerably cheaper than the next lowest.

Contractually Rutland had the choice to stand by their tender or withdraw. Senior managers and directors from the building group and housing met to discuss the issue and without consideration of the fact the building group had to make a profit to exist it was decided they should do the work which would inevitably lead to their closure. Those responsible for this decision should be ashamed of themselves because it meant as a consequence about twenty five people lost their jobs unnecessarily.

Initially a small office was set up to run the job with a new contracts manager called Fred Baker who was previously assistant head Q.S. of the building group at the main depot and a Q.S. who came from William's office. The contract period was three years, so at least they had secured that amount of employment, but the job was difficult and they were loosing money from day one.

Then a drastic and ruthless event occurred. Fred Baker approached the director of building and made a suggestion that the Craig Estate contract should merge with the building group and he should take over as contracts manager.

The building group was a successful unit making money and it was obviously his idea to cream some of this off to support Craig Estate. But what eventually happened was the whole unit made a loss and was closed down. So Fred had muscled his way in and pushed a popular contracts manager out, he was disliked by the entire department.

William felt reasonably secure under the previous manager, but was now worried about his position. The question was could he get on with Fred? During the change over William had taken a couple of weeks holiday with his wife in a caravan at Hunstanton on the Norfolk coast and returned refreshed not knowing what to expect. Fred was broad shouldered and threw his weight around a bit, so William decided to lie low and tread the ground carefully.

Before this event occurred William had been given a job which had come from another building department at the main depot. It was supposed to have been carried out by the direct labour organisation (d.l.o.) but the surveyor was having difficulties when the roofer on one of the two properties withdrew.

So the job was dumped on his desk for him to sort out. It was the refurbishment of two dwellings and had a contract value of £150,000. It was intended that the work on the more straight forward house without the re-roofing should be carried out by the d.l.o. and the other would be subcontracted out into various work packages, which is what happened.

William put the roofing out to tender and took on the best contractor who had submitted the lowest price. The scaffolding was erected and works proceeded internally in the large five bedroom dwelling. The flank wall was leaning outwards and had to be tied in with metal to the first floor joists.

A lot of the timber was rotten and had to be renewed. The sash windows were carefully made up by a local reputable joiner at a very reasonable price and fitted by Jimmy Reed, a good Irish subcontractor who also carried out most of the general building work which included cutting out unstable brickwork on the internal skin and plastering.

Most of the houses built around 1900 have a one brick wall; cavity wall construction was not introduced until later. A skilled apprentice served bricklayer would lay the external skin and usually the internal skin was laid by an apprentice or labourer because this would be hidden by the plaster and more often than not it was of very poor quality. This led to internal cracks where the brickwork was not bonded very well and when the plaster had been removed it revealed the shoddy workmanship.

A new vinyl floor finish was laid in the kitchen, complete with worktops and wall tiling. The bathroom was tiled throughout having fitted a new toilet and basin with pedal stool. The house was completely rewired and a new central heating system was fitted. Also the old external drainage had to be broken up and a new system was laid.

Towards the end of the works Fred Baker sacked the full time site agent because he felt he was dragging his heals, the job was running well over the contract period. William asked Fred who would replace him and he said there wouldn't be a replacement and he expected William to run the job on site as well.

This was all part of Fred's thinning out strategy, the site agent was not very good anyway, he used to spend hours talking in the office spinning yarns about what a marvellous job he had done on previous contracts in this country and abroad in Africa and quite frankly he drove everybody up the wall. So he wasn't missed, but nevertheless his departure was worrying, who would be next in the firing line?

William kept his nose clean and despite encouragement from the other surveyors to stand his ground and refuse to run the job because he was a Q.S. and not a site agent; he did as he was told otherwise he might have been the next person to go. So he caught a train and had a twenty minute walk to the site on a fairly regular basis to keep an eye on things and direct the labour accordingly. The other dwelling which was run entirely by the d.l.o. was also running over time and seriously over budget which was not a worry for William because that responsibility lied with the other building group.

There was one thing the previous site agent had overlooked and that was the flue which should have been fitted in the fireplace in the front room which had been bricked in. Fortunately William picked up on this just before the scaffolding was due to be removed. Once the decorating was completed the house was handed over and was soon occupied by a large young family.

It was around this time that William developed a problem with his gall bladder and was patiently waiting on the list to go into Colchester General Hospital to have it removed. One evening at home he drank a little too much rum having received a large bill for the window replacement in his flat and the next day was very ill.

He was taken to Guys Hospital where he was given a pain killer and was recommended bed rest. He stayed there for a few hours and then went home and took a couple of days off to rest.

The long hours travelling and the pressures of work and his gall bladder problem were telling on him. He was so glad when they took him into hospital and had it removed by keyhole surgery. But a stone had dropped out during surgery and was trapped in his bile duct. This was removed after two attempts by passing a pipe through the mouth to the duct while under sedation.

After four weeks William was back at work felling much better. Fred had him earmarked for doing small jobs running them on site as well. One of these was a drainage contract walking distance from the office. The job entailed excavating and breaking out the existing drainage and laying the new alongside two adjacent blocks of flats.

The job was reasonably straight forward but unfortunately the excavator dug up some B.T. cables which were not clearly marked on the drawings and B.T. made a bit of a meal with their charges. William argued with them, they went to Rutland's insurance section and it came back down the line and he had to pay them and deduct the sum from the subcontractor's payment. He was not pleased because he knew that B.T. had overstated the number of hours they claimed to have worked on the job, but he was powerless to do anything about it.

CHAPTER V1

William had had a lot of experience in the refurbishment and alteration to existing buildings, particularly houses and he expressed his interest to Fred who managed to secure a contract for four terraced houses. These houses were in a very sad state and it would have been better to knock them down and start again. But rebuilding came from a different housing budget and there was no money there so they had to be renovated. The bill had been priced without going out to tender, so William had the job of preparing the documents and going out to five carefully selected contractors.

In preparing the documents William noticed that they had not got an item for scaffolding so he included this item in the contractors brief and wrote to the architect stating there would be this additional cost. Fred said it was probably included in the preliminaries somewhere, William knew it wasn't.

When the architect wrote back and asked what this additional cost would be Fred said 'William, let me shake you by the hand'. When the tenders came back in and William had selected the lowest, he knew what the scaffolding cost would be and added on a sizeable proportion and submitted this price to the architect.

The works soon got underway, a port cabin was set up on site to be used as a site hut and mess room for the subcontractors. A site agent was assigned full time to the job who was a carpenter by trade and ideal for the task. He had a chat with William one day on site and noticing how tired he was suggested that he found accommodation in London during the week to relieve him of all the travelling.

They looked through the local paper and found a suitable place to stay. The landlord was an Irishman who had lost his wife; he had his own business as a ground worker. They got on very well and the rent was very reasonable. There were two other lodgers and they all shared the same kitchen which wasn't a problem. It was good to get plenty of rest in the evening, but he did miss his wife and the home comforts.

There were certain people in Rutland's architects and surveyors department who didn't like Rutland Construction and the contact administrator on this job was one of those. He wasn't very good at his job and tried to point the finger at the contractor when things started to go wrong and tended to back away from making decisions letting the contractor go ahead as they saw fit then blaming them if things go quite right. Written instructions were few and far between, which made things difficult at valuation time.

The subcontractor was aware of the beast and they covered themselves by getting the site agent to sign any verbal instructions to ensure they got paid. So, as is quite often the case, the main contractor (Rutland Construction) was very much 'piggy in the middle', making authorisations for work to be done and hoping that this work would be confirmed by way of an instruction.

All the floor boards had to be renewed because they were rotten and the ground was excavated and levelled and new support brick piers were built. The brickwork was in a terrible state and a lot of it had to be rebuilt. A previous contractor had renewed a flank wall without bonding in the brickwork and it was leaning dangerously outwards. The contract administrator met this contractor on site to discuss this issue, but he wasn't even capable of sorting it out properly and just let the contractor's representative do all the talking and managed to get away with the dreadful work they had done.

A risk assessment and method statement had to be drawn up before works could proceed. The upper part of the wall was shored up with three sets of pins holding it up while the lower wall was broken out and rebuilt, this time being bonded into the facing wall. Then the remaining upper wall was carefully renewed one course at a time.

Most of the concrete window sills were renewed by breaking out the old, forming timber formwork, and then pouring the concrete levelling the top and striking the formwork to leave the desired finish. The site agent seemed to be busy doing some of the carpentry work as well as looking after the site. No doubt he had a private financial arrangement with the subcontractor which William chose to turn a blind eye to rather than make an issue of it because he got on well with him and he did a good job.

This was a major refurbishment contract and fortunately the subcontractor was a good one who knew what was required and guided the administrator accordingly who wasn't up to the job. William's counterpart, the client's Q.S. was equally inexperienced and only attended site one a month on valuation day which wasn't helpful. He only paid for work done that had a written instruction which made things difficult because as previously stated the instructions were not very forthcoming.

There was a lot of correspondence from William and Fred stating all the extra work which had not got an instruction, some of which was later confirmed, but there was a horrible worrying time lag. This made William's job more complex and it was usually difficult to balance what was coming in with his payments going out. He was shrewd and had allowed a sufficient mark up to adequately compensate for this leaving a reasonable profit margin.

Early on in the contract the site hut was completely burnt out by vandals. Fortunately William kept his paperwork in the main office, but all the site agent's instructions and drawings were destroyed. William had duplicate copies so this wasn't a problem. The replacement hut was armoured and vandal proof and there were no further occurrences of this nature.

A meeting was arranged on site with the subcontractor and his surveyor and William to discuss a few monetary issues. The main item on the agenda was the extra dubbing out of plasterwork required so that the walls were square. But as William clearly said it was stated in the documents under the description for plastering that the rate should include for all necessary dubbing out.

The surveyor was a pompous twit and a member of the Royal Institute of Chartered Surveyors and he kept on and on about how much more they had to do than expected. Furthermore, he claimed they had a similar situation with another London Borough who agreed to pay them extra. William said that was a different contract with probably a varying description and therefore bore no comparison. Even if the particulars were similar or the same he disagreed with their decision and stood firm with what he thought was right.

William also commented that he was surprised that a surveyor of his standing and supposed experience was putting so much emphasis on this particular issue which clearly stated the scope of the work adequately and therefore their obligation.

The meeting ended with a few steamed up red faces. They had failed to capitalise on what they saw was a loophole in the documents. William felt quite stressed yet also relieved that the meeting was over and that he had prevented a golden opportunity for the subcontractor to make a lot of money because the thickness of the dubbing out would be very difficult to verify now this part of the work was complete.

Also, the chances are the client's surveyor would have the same opinion as William so they wouldn't get paid anyway. William didn't go down the dangerous road of trying to claim for this item and not passing it on. He considered that to be unethical.

The finished job looked a treat. All houses had new bathroom and kitchen units and two houses had extensions built on the back. The gardens were laid to turf and were divided by neat timber fencing. The transformation was quite remarkable, a credit to the builder. Also William made a tidy profit which pleased Fred, but this was being swallowed up the dreadful loses on the Craig Estate project.

It is common for quantity surveyors to have three or four jobs running at the same time, generally at different stages. Naturally the number of jobs was dependant on size and complexity, for example Craig Estate had one surveyor full time.

William was also working on a large school called St. Martins which was for primary and junior children; it had four floors and an annex for the disabled and was so large that in the main building there were coloured lines for certain classes painted on the floor for the children to follow so they wouldn't get lost.

The contract was for the external painting of both blocks, re roofing of the annex's pitched roof and resurfacing the main building's flat roof with tarmac. Also the external stonework had to be chemically cleaned which raised a few health and safety issues.

Once the scaffolding was up the first job was to clean the stonework and while this was being done the roofers started to strip the roof of tiles on the annex. Then the preparation for painting began, starting at the top and working down.

The roofers were a good team consisting of three brothers and two others. The contract administrator was a bit out of his depth and when they came across a detail problem in a valley there was a meeting on the roof with him, a clerk of works, a product representative, the site agent and two roofers. All in all a combination of over fifty years experience trying to advise him of a solution and he still couldn't make up his mind.

When painting, windows have to be opened which requires access to the building. This isn't a problem in normal school hours, but out of hours like earlier in the morning and weekends a school attendant has to be present. This was the school caretaker and William kept a record of these extra hours so he could be paid overtime.

But when William was informed by the subcontractor that the caretaker was also requesting a backhander for access from them, he was extremely annoyed. He was being greedy and obviously enjoying the surplus money because he had red glazed eyes from drinking too much whiskey. The job was running very well and William chose not to rock the boat by reporting him.

It is written into the contract that any materials found on the site shall be the property of the employer. During the roofing works two lovely old terracotta chimney pots were taken down because they were no longer required. So they should have been the property of the school, but they weren't informed. The site agent had one and the supervising officer the other. This sort of thing occurs a lot in building and is considered as a perk for the more senior members of the team.

The site agent was an aggressive man in his mid fifties and wasn't shy about receiving the odd backhander, which is probably why William didn't get on with him. But he had his good points, the site was clean and tidy and well organised.

Furthermore, his paperwork was good, keeping an up to date record of all the site activities and making sure any extra work over and above that originally specified or instructed was written out on a standard confirmation of verbal instruction sheet and signed by the supervising officer so that at a later stage it could be raised as an architects instruction to enable payment.

The paint system was a standard wash and rub down of loose and flaking paint, prime bare timber, then two undercoats and one gloss coat with paint acceptable to the supervising officer. The site agent had his wits about him and insisted that the two undercoats should be a different colour so he could be sure the painters didn't claim they had applied two coats instead of one.

The roof of the main building was flat and had a football pitch marked out on it. But it had not been used for many years because the access door was firmly locked at all times. The tarmac was stripped and relayed in bays. Access was by way of a hoist and all the material had to be painstakingly barrowed up.

But a good job was done with only one hiccup. The plumber forgot to cap of some pipe work which was used to supply water for the works and over the weekend the roof flooded and seeped through the building much to their embarrassment. The damage was assessed and the subcontractor had to pay the cost to make good through his insurers.

The job finished on time and William made a reasonable profit. Moreover, the school were very pleased with the end product and complimented the main contractor on how amicable and courteous they had been throughout the contract especially in working around their needs.

CHAPTER V11

A convenient job that William acquired was situated at the back of his site office. The scope of the works was window replacement, concrete repairs, asbestos removal and painting to a four storey block of flats. The asbestos was a sheet lining under the existing windows at the front of the building.

In accordance with health and safety requirements a method statement and risk analysis had to be drawn up by the specialist subcontractor carry out this item of work. This had to be forwarded to the supervising officer for his approval before the work could commence.

Asbestos is a hazardous material and before it could be touched the surrounding area had to be tented out to contain all dust particles. The work was carried out in stages working in coordination with the window fixers so a void was not left for any length of time. This was agreed at pre contract stage so they were fully aware of their obligation when pricing their tender. Otherwise they would almost certainly put in a claim for more money for working out of sequence unproductively.

The concrete repairs were to the main structural frame of the building. A lot of flats were built in this manner in the sixties. It was the intention of the supervising officer to include the painting of these concrete surfaces in the bill of quantities. But in the description it said to paint previously painted surfaces, but the concrete was not previously painted, which had been overlooked by the client's Q.S. when preparing the documents.

The painting subcontractor raised this issue with William who asked for their price for preparing the surface and painting with three coats of fine textured masonry paint having indicated to the supervising officer that there would be this additional cost. He raised an architect's instruction for this work and William submitted his price having enhanced the subcontractor's price quite considerably to increase his profit margin.

The window subcontractor was a big problem. They had done several jobs very well for Rutland in the past, but not this one. They appeared to have a dreadful shortage of window fixers and those few on site were a bad crew. Furthermore, to make matters worse, the site agent was having some personal problems and as a consequence didn't seem to care and was not looking after the job properly.

The clerk of the works had a bad report by phone from one of the residents and went to the site to investigate. The fixers were taking out the old windows and leaving the waste materials piled up dangerously on the scaffolding and not disposing into the waste skips. The site agent was nowhere to be seen so the clerk called on William and advised him that he wanted works to stop until the hazardous mess had been cleared. Neither Fred nor the contracts manager was contactable so William had to attend site and deal with the matter.

This is just one example of the problems they were causing, in fact their attendance and workmanship was so bad that William deducted monies from their payments. At the end of the job William and the contracts manager went to the subcontractor's office at Fred's request to agree the final account.

It is an unusual procedure to go to a subcontractor's office at their request, usually they are asked to go to the main contractor's office but this is not always the case. To make things more difficult it was suspected that Fred had a cosy relationship with them. As a consequence of their poor performance William had blown them out on their tender on a bigger job that was starting up, which they were not happy about at all. There had been rumours that the founder of the company had a dodgy background with the wide boys in London, which was distasteful.

All's well that ends well, as they say. William made over £100,000 profit on the job which pleased Fred no end. This margin was made possible by extra works and a good relationship with the client's Q.S. who was very laid back. The neighbourhood were very pleased with the end product which was a bonus.

Another job that William got involved with was the re roofing of an eight storey block of flats. The area was felted on top of layers of insulation. The other tenders for the job had allowed for full scaffolding all round. But William invited a scaffolding subcontractor to attend site to see if a cantilever type of guard rail around the perimeter of the roof could be temporarily fixed, and it could. This made a huge saving on the job.

The architect was a pompous individual who was seeing out time before moving onto another job. The design services had already been paid for a ridiculous design of fixing a pitched roof, which was elaborate and unworkable.

But the job went reasonably well apart from one hiccup. The insulation fixers were not supposed to leave any unfixed material on the roof overnight. But they did one Friday night and what's more they didn't tie it down. William knew the site agent was not on site at the end of the day because he had called into the office in the middle of the afternoon to get his timesheet signed and then cleared of home. But he swore blind he was there till the end of the day and had made sure the material had been securely tied down.

There were high winds that weekend and some sheets of insulation blew off the roof. Thank God they didn't hit anybody otherwise all hell would have been let loose. William didn't grass the agent up but from that day on he had a poor opinion of him.

Concrete repair jobs were quite common in the office. This work was carried out in conjunction with other works like window replacement and painting. William had one or two other such like jobs on high rise blocks which went according to plan without any problems.

William was given a £150,000 painting and associated repairs job which involved several blocks of flats. The subcontractor was new to their list and he had submitted a very cheap tender. In fact it was too cheap and after two and a half months suddenly withdrew. They were naturally taken off their list of subcontractors who were invited to tender for future jobs.

This left the organisation and William with a problem because most of the blocks had been started and only a few were completed. William needed to act quickly, re tendering was too slow because they had to complete the job within the contract period. The only way out was to assign a contractor on a day work basis which is a method where the labour is paid an hourly rate and the materials are also paid for.

The problem with day work is that there is no cost control because the labour is not held to a price. They get paid for the number of hours they attend and work regardless of how productive they are. Unfortunately this reduced the profit margin on the job. Three subcontractors were invited to submit their rates and the cheapest was taken on.

There was a small delay in the works and it ran over the contract period but the client didn't deduct any monies for damages. William was just glad to see this job done and dusted and out the way. It's always a difficult situation when a subcontractor withdraws, especially when they tender to carry out all the works.

A huge job came into the office and William volunteered to be the surveyor. He had a three week run in period before the job was due to start. This was valuable time to sort through his subcontractors and negotiate lower prices. The job involved renewing lift shafts, re roofing, window replacement and painting of three blocks of flats. The contract sum was £1.2 million.

The lowest window replacement subcontractor tender William had already had a bad experience with, so he blew them out and negotiated a lower price with a more reputable organisation. There was an opportunity to make a large saving on the protective scaffolding covering to the roof. William spoke to a helpful scaffolding company who came up with a Japanese idea called a Haki system. This consisted of a scaffold around the perimeter of the roof and some supports at intervals along the roof for large sheets of polythene held taut with timber around the outside. These would be moved along the roof when required as work proceeded. This was much cheaper than a conventional temporary structure.

Having a temporary roof cover was necessary to protect the building from rain while carrying out the roofing works. There had been another job in the office where this had not been allowed for in the tender which resulted in rain water entering the dwellings. The occupants claimed against Rutland Construction which gave serious losses on the job. It stated in the contract that the contractor was responsible for the building during the contract period, so Rutland were unable to claim these monies back from the client.

CHAPTER V111

All in all things were going very well for William, perhaps too well. He was earning more money for the company than any other surveyor and enjoying his work also. But things came down with an almighty crash. He had been working too hard and had a nervous breakdown.

This was a problem that William knew from the past and the horrible beast had reared its ugly head again. He had taken medication daily for a condition of paranoia and schizophrenia for a long time and he hadn't had an occurrence for over fifteen years. In fact this period of time had been so long that he thought these problems were over with, but not so.

He went back to Colchester with his wife and was admitted into hospital for care. He spent three months there and had a further couple of weeks off, then gradually went back to work a few days at a time. But unfortunately he wasn't the same person and he found he couldn't concentrate properly. He was given light work to start with, but he was struggling.

The Craig Estate contract came to an end and made a bad loss as expected. The money made on the other contracts was insufficient to balance the books so the department made a loss. The director held a meeting with all the employees and told them it was his decision to close the building department down. This had been on the cards for a long time, but William was glad because once again he was finding the travelling and work very tiring.

About eighteen months previously William was fortunate enough to have been taken on the cards as a full time employee. He was pleased because it meant more money and holiday entitlement. Fred had decided to offer contracts to three surveyors because it was cheaper as the company didn't have to pay the agency fees.

William managed to secure further work and was the last employee to leave having just completed two years of his contract which entitled him to a small redundancy package and a pension when he retired. He worked for a short period of time but found things increasingly difficult due to poor health.

He qualified for disability living allowance and incapacity benefit and although his physical health gradually became worse his mental health improved. He now enjoys his early retirement pursuing his interests in woodwork, collecting vinyl records, oil painting and writing.

www.ingramcontent.com/pod-product-compliance
Ingram Content Group UK Ltd.
Pitfield, Milton Keynes, MK11 3LW, UK
UKHW041228200426
11947UKWH00034B/427